A Hungry Day
at the Corner Cafe

By D.C. Abbott

**Illustrated by
John Steven Gurney**

To KYLE
&
MELANIE
BEST
WISHES!
JOHN
STEVEN
GURNEY

Design and production by BIG BLUE DOT

Cover photography by Sandra Kimball

03 02 01 00 99 98 97   10 9 8 7 6 5 4 3 2

Library of Congress Catalog Card Number 96-85701

ISBN 1-889514-00-4

It was time for breakfast, and Nibble
was hungry. He headed for the Corner Cafe,
Hudson Hill's favorite restaurant.

3

"Hello," said Galena, the owner of the cafe. "Welcome to the Corner Cafe."

4

Galena showed Nibble to a table. "Have a seat," she said. And she pulled out a chair. "Here's a menu," she added. "Your waiter will be with you soon."

Then she hurried off to greet another customer.

Carlyle came up to the table. "Good morning," he said. "My name is Carlyle, and I'll be your waiter."

"Good morning," said Nibble. "My name is Nibble, and I'm really hungry."

"Then you're in the right place," said Carlyle. "Ace, our chef, is the best cook in town."

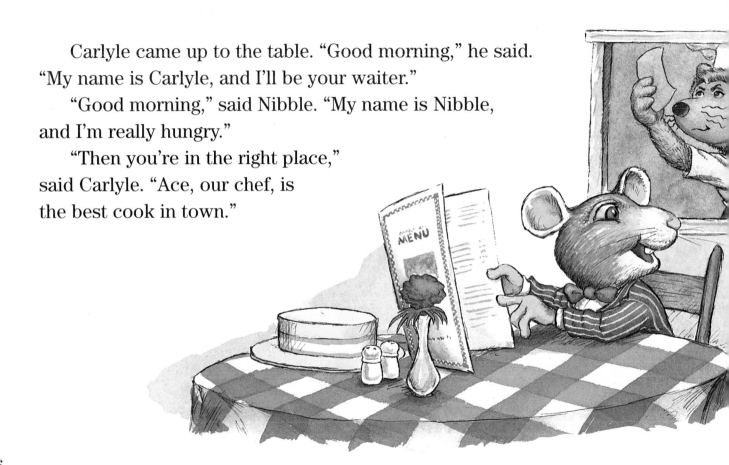

He went on, "What would you like today? I recommend the banana pancakes. They're one of Ace's specialties."

"Banana pancakes sound delicious," said Nibble. "And I'll have scrambled eggs and toast and cereal and juice too."

Carlyle stared at the tiny mouse. Then he started to write on his order pad. "Coming right up," he said.

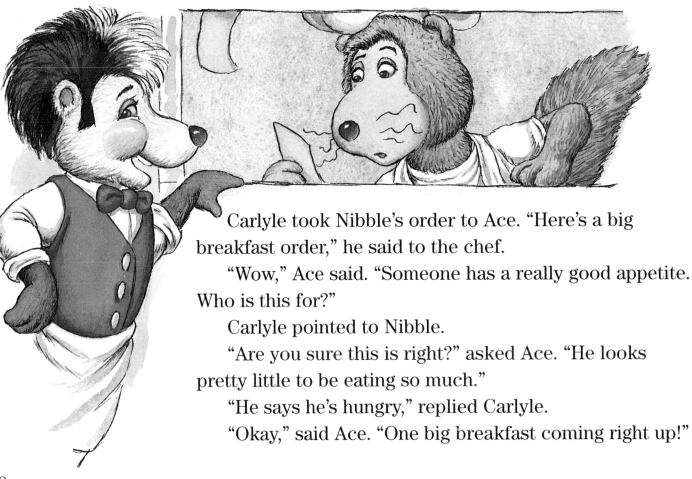

Carlyle took Nibble's order to Ace. "Here's a big breakfast order," he said to the chef.

"Wow," Ace said. "Someone has a really good appetite. Who is this for?"

Carlyle pointed to Nibble.

"Are you sure this is right?" asked Ace. "He looks pretty little to be eating so much."

"He says he's hungry," replied Carlyle.

"Okay," said Ace. "One big breakfast coming right up!"

Ace got busy. He mixed banana pancake batter. He scrambled eggs. He toasted bread. He filled a bowl with cereal and poured orange juice into a glass.

Then Ace put everything on a tray. "That's some breakfast!" he said. He peeked out the window. The little mouse still looked little. But he also looked hungry.

"Order's ready," Ace called to Carlyle.

Carlyle picked up the tray. It was heavy! He hurried to Nibble's table. "Here's your breakfast," he said as he arranged the dishes in front of the mouse. "Enjoy it."

"Yum," said Nibble. And he started to eat.

While he waited on his other customers, Carlyle watched the little mouse. The pancakes disappeared. The eggs disappeared. The toast and cereal and juice disappeared.

Carlyle hurried over to the table. "Can I get you anything else?" he asked.

"No thanks," said Nibble. "That was wonderful. My compliments to the chef." He wiped his mouth carefully with his napkin.

11

Carlyle put Nibble's bill on the table. "Thanks for coming," he said. "Come back soon."

"I will," said Nibble. And he left two quarters on the table for Carlyle's tip.

At the cash register, Galena looked at the bill. She looked at Nibble. "Was everything okay?" she asked.

"Delicious. Absolutely delicious!" responded Nibble.

"Come back soon," said Galena as the mouse left.

"I will!" he called.

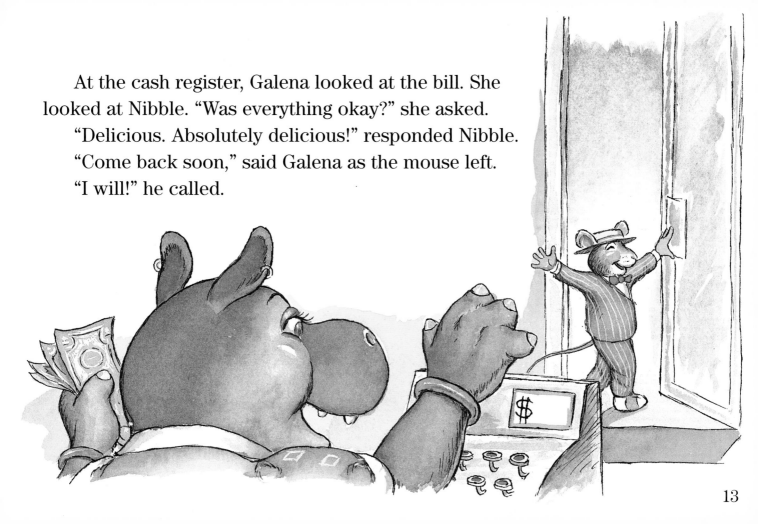

Soon breakfast was over. Galena straightened up the menus. She counted the money in the cash register. Then she made a sign for the lunch specials.

"It was a busy morning," she said to Carlyle.

"It sure was," answered Carlyle as he cleared off tables. "And we had some really hungry customers."

Carlyle took the dirty dishes to Ace. Then he got the tables ready for lunch.

In the kitchen, Ace washed the breakfast dishes. Then he started to get things ready for lunch.

Soon the lunch rush started. There were customers everywhere. "Please take a seat. Have a menu," Galena said over and over again.

"What would you like today?" Carlyle asked customer after customer.

"Order's ready!" Ace called again and again.

And then—in walked Nibble.

"Welcome back," said Galena.

"Thanks," said Nibble. "Breakfast was so delicious that I decided to have lunch here too."

Galena couldn't believe the little mouse had any room left for lunch, but she didn't say anything.

"Welcome back," said Carlyle when he came up to Nibble's table. He couldn't believe the mouse was back either. He asked, "Would you like to order some lunch?"

"I certainly would," said Nibble. "I'm starving! What do you recommend?"

Nibble ordered a grilled cheese sandwich, just like Carlyle recommended. And then he ordered tomato soup, a salad, milk, french fries, and pineapple upside-down cake.

Carlyle wrote and wrote. Then he took the order to Ace.

"A big lunch order," Carlyle called out. Ace looked at the order. "I'll say," he commented. "Who's this for, an elephant?"

"Guess again," said Carlyle. He whispered in Ace's ear. Ace peeked at Nibble and shook his head.

19

So Ace made grilled cheese and soup
and salad and pineapple upside-down cake.
He put it all on a tray with french fries and
a glass of milk.

Carlyle took everything to his customer. And Nibble started to eat. He ate and he ate.

Before long, Nibble was the only customer left in the restaurant. Carlyle cleared off all the other tables. Ace washed the dishes and cleaned up the kitchen. And still Nibble ate.

21

Finally Nibble finished the last bite of food. He took his bill to the cash register and gave his money to Galena.

"Thanks for coming," said Galena.

"Good-bye, Nibble," called Carlyle.

"Good-bye," said the little mouse. He waved a tiny paw and went out the door.

Ace came out of the kitchen. "I don't think we'll see him again soon," he commented. "It'll be days before he's hungry."

Carlyle and Galena nodded in agreement.

But just then, the cafe door opened again. Nibble stuck his head in.

"Oh, I forgot to ask," he said. "What time do you open for dinner?"

24